Time for a HOLIDAY

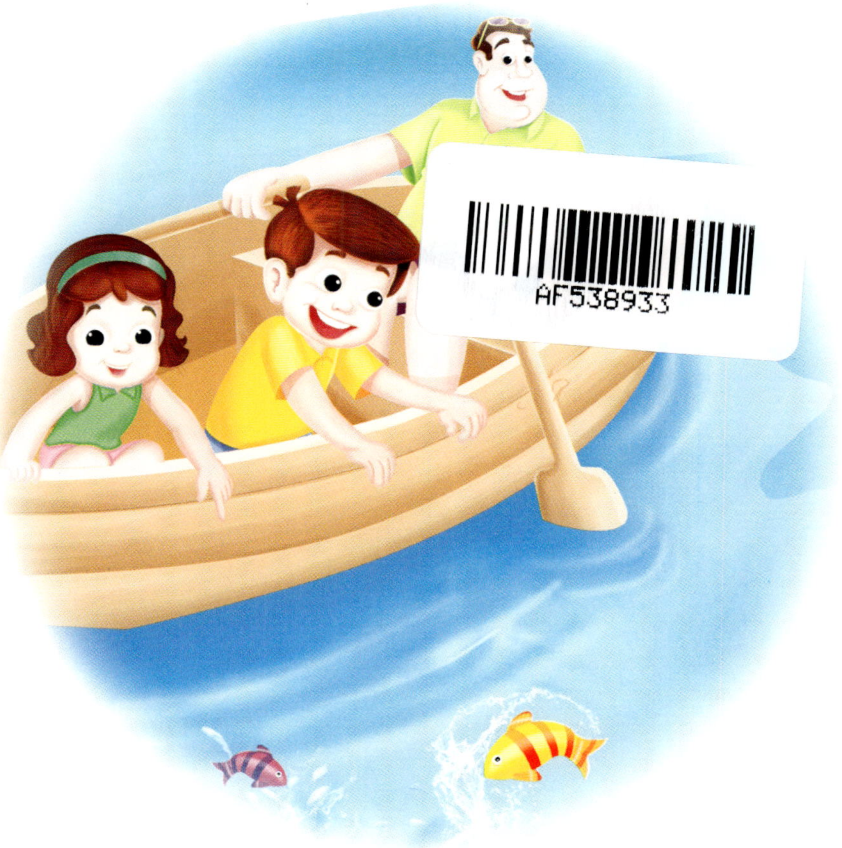

Om KIDZ
An imprint of Om Books International

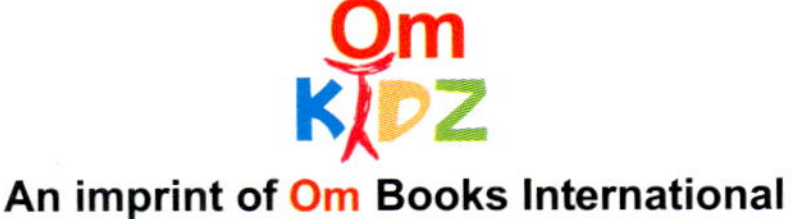

Reprinted in 2025

Corporate & Editorial Office
A-12, Sector 64, Noida 201 301
Uttar Pradesh, India
Phone: +91 120 477 4100
Email: editorial@ombooks.com
Website: www.ombooksinternational.com

Sales Office
107, Ansari Road, Darya Ganj
New Delhi 110 002, India
Phone: +91 11 4000 9000
Email: sales@ombooks.com
Website: www.ombooks.com

ISBN: 978-93-86108-22-7

Printed in India

10 9 8 7 6 5 4 3

Time for a HOLIDAY

I'm all set to read

Paste your photograph here

My name is

Amy and Ben are going on a holiday. Their **dad** is taking them to a tiny town by **the sea**. They **are** going to stay in a cottage by **the** beach.

HONK! HONK!

Dad is waiting in **the car**. **Amy and Ben hop** into **the car and** go **for** their holiday.

After **two** hours, they reach **the** cottage.

“**Wow**, what a lovely cottage!” says **Amy**. **She** can’t wait to **see** what’s inside.

"**Let**'s **put our** bags in **and get** some food from town," says **Dad**. **Amy and Ben nod** hungrily.

They go to town **and** find a cosy **inn**. **Dad** orders an **egg and ham** sandwich. **Amy** gets pancakes. **Ben** gets a **big** slice of cherry **pie**.

They **eat** their food **and** return to **the** cottage. "Time **for bed**!" says **Dad**. He tucks them in **and** says goodnight. "**Let** us go fishing tomorrow!" he says.

"**YES**!" **the** children squeal with **joy**.

The next **day**, **Dad** wakes them up early. They **get** into a boat **and row** into **the sea**.

“Look at **all** those fishes!” says **Ben**. “Give me **the** fishing **rod**.”

Dad checks **the bag** he brought along. It **has** a **mat**. It **has** a **can** of worms. It even **has** a **net**. **But** he does **not see** a **rod**.

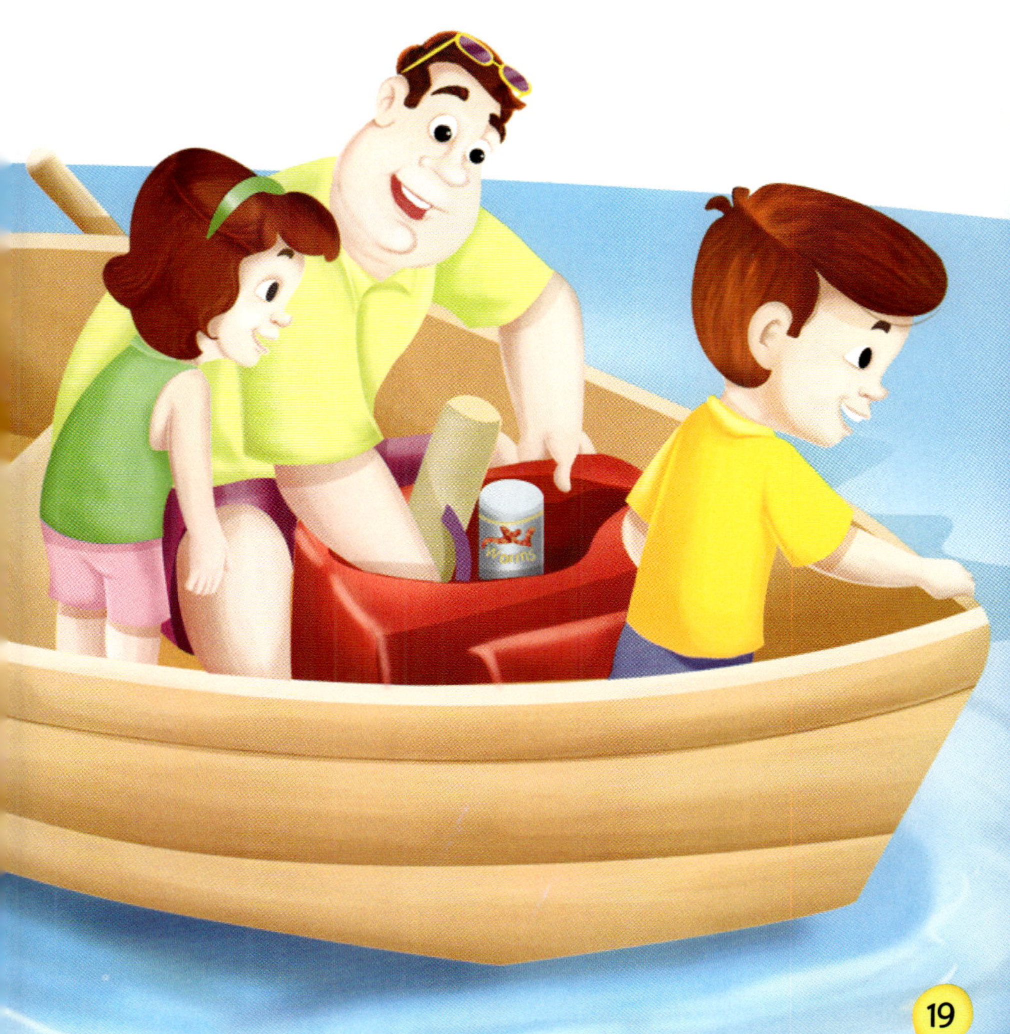

"Uh oh!" says **Dad**. "I forgot to **get the rod**. **But** we have a **net**."

"**Let** us **use the net**!" says **Amy**.

Dad brings **out the net and** casts it into **the sea**.

Dad, **Ben and Amy** fish **all** morning. They catch **ten big** fish in **the net**.

But Amy feels sorry **for the** fish. So, **Dad** lets **all the** fish back into **the sea**.

They return to **the** cottage.

They **all** have a nice dinner.

They **eat** a **bun** each. There **are** nice **red** tomatoes **too**. **And** they **all** have a **big** plate of pasta.

They **all dig** into a delicious meal.

Amy, **Ben and Dad** spend a **fun** week by **the sea**. They swim in **the sea**. They sing songs **and** tell stories. Soon, it is time to go home.

"This **was** such a lovely holiday," says **Amy**. "I wish we could come here every year."

"Oh, **but** we should," says **Ben**.

"**And** we will!" says **Dad**. **The** children thank **him** with a **big hug**.

Unscramble the letters and make words!

Circle the boats with three-letter words.

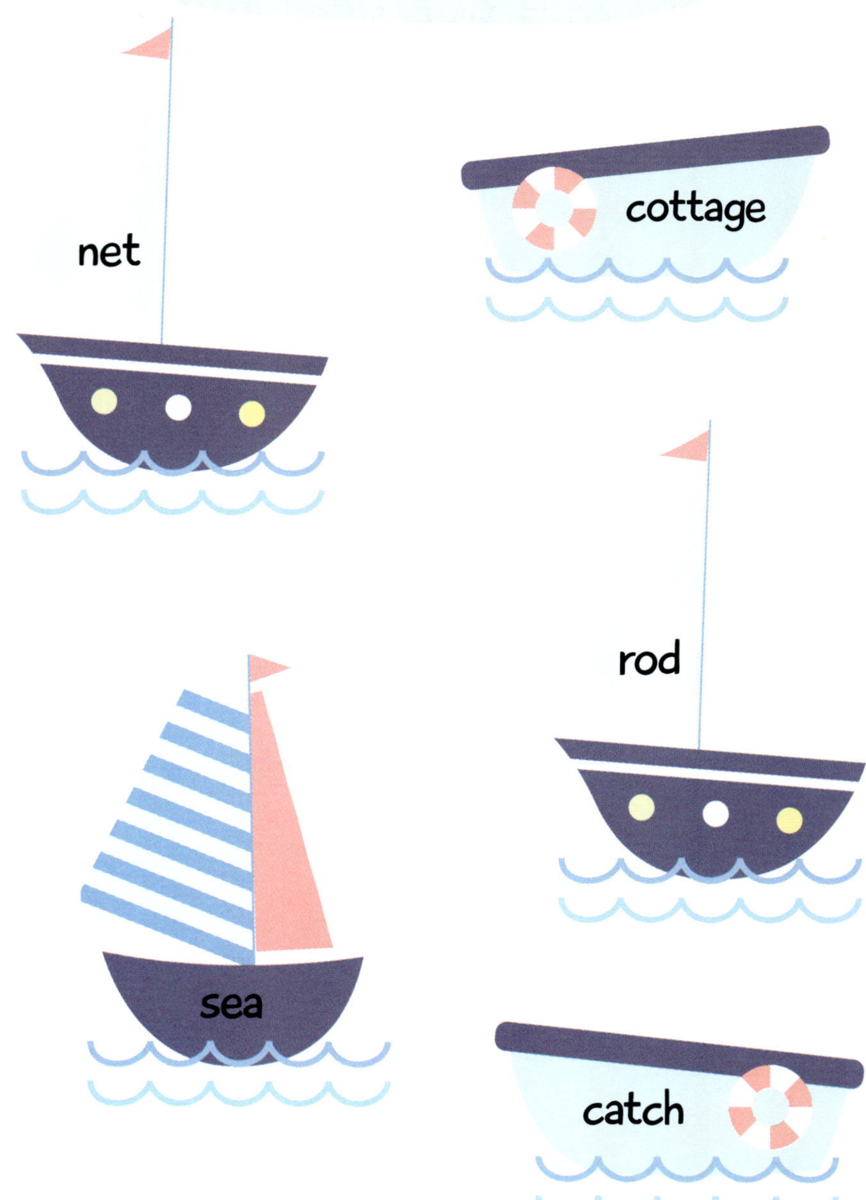

How many fish did Amy, Ben and Dad catch? Colour the correct number.

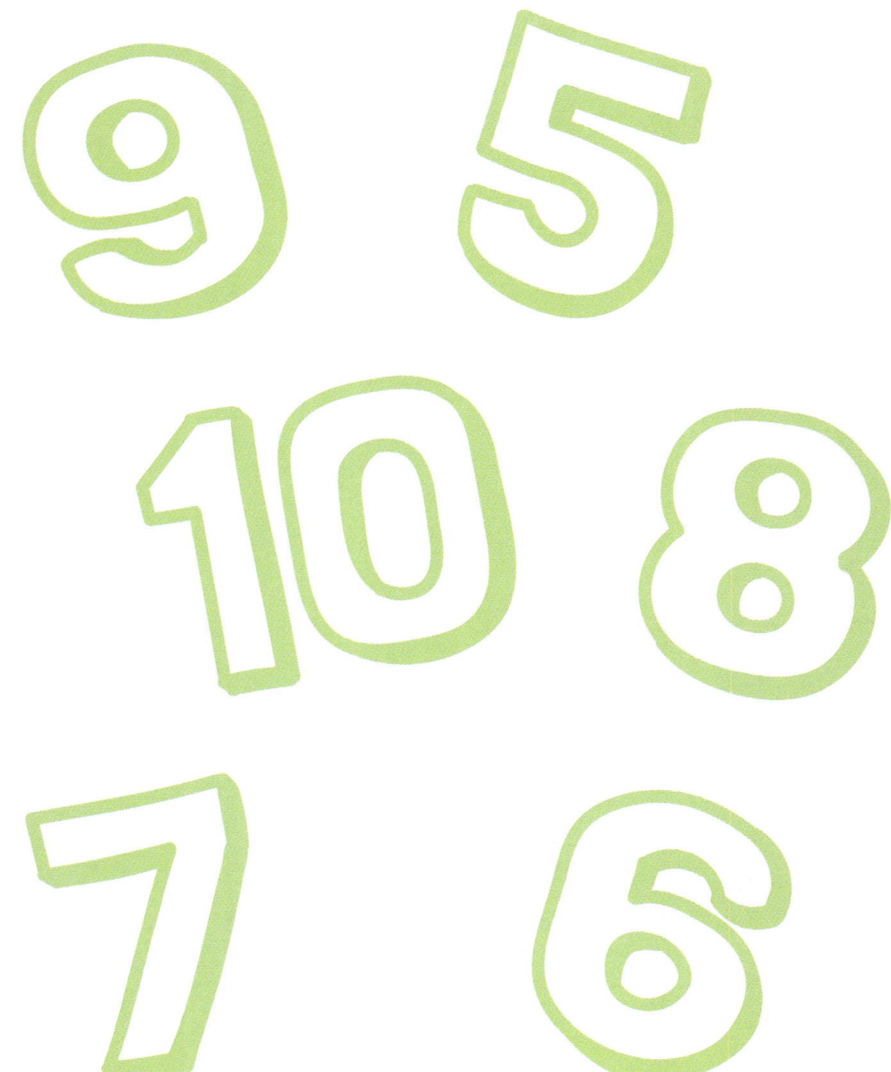

Know your words

Sight Words

the	our	fun	ten
are	out	joy	red
and	let	all	too
for	nod	has	was
two	big	but	him
wow	yes	not	
she	day	use	

Naming Words

Amy	car	pie	mat
Ben	inn	bed	can
Dad	egg	rod	net
sea	ham	bag	bun

Doing Words

hop	put	eat	row
hug	get	dig	see